OPPOSITES
ABSTRACT

BY MO WILLEMS

HYPERION BOOKS FOR CHILDREN / NEW YORK

IS THIS
DARK?

IS THIS
LIGHT?

IS THIS
SOFT?

IS THIS HARD

IS THIS
MECHANICAL?

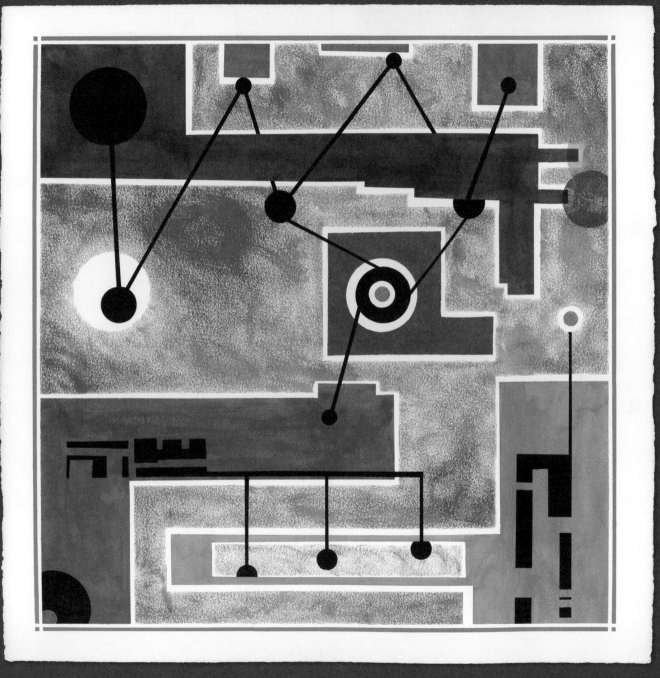

IS THIS
ORGANIC?

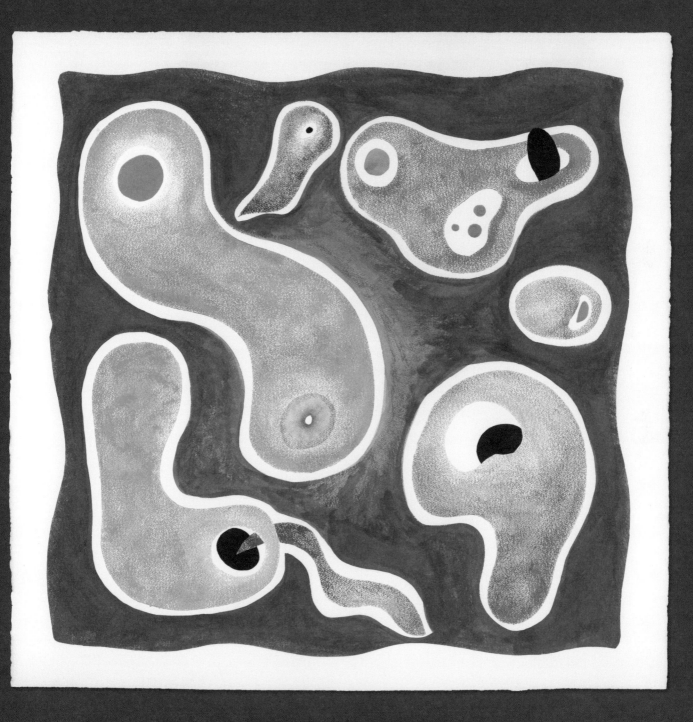

IS THIS AN
INDIVIDUAL?

ARE THESE
GROUPS?

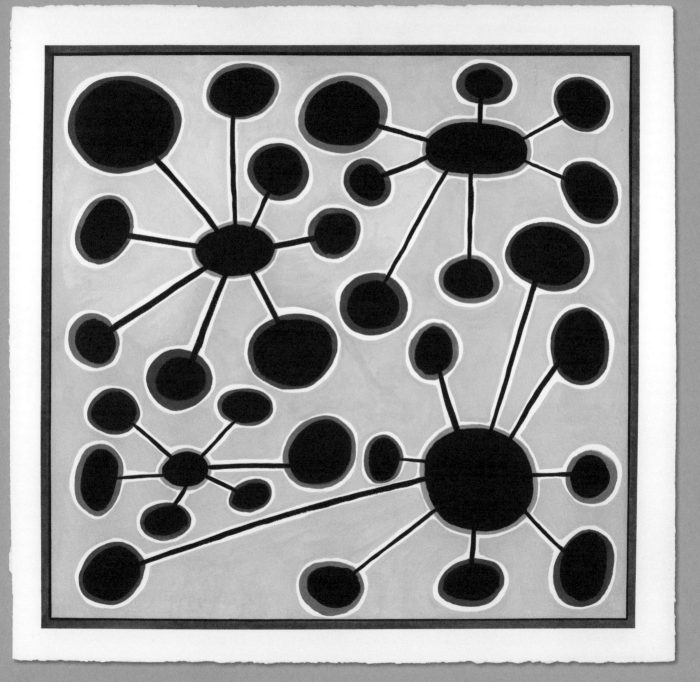

IS THIS **INCLUSION?**

IS THIS
INTENTIONAL?

IS THIS
ACCIDENTAL?

IS THIS
BROKEN?

IS THIS
FIXED?

IS THIS
CALM?

IS THIS
EXCITED?

IS THIS AWAKE?

IS THIS
ASLEEP?

THIS IS **FINISHED.**